Rabén & Sjögren Bokförlag, Stockholm
http://www.raben.se

Translation copyright © 2001 by Rabén & Sjögren Bokförlag
Text copyright © 2000 by Lena Arro
Pictures copyright © 2000 by Catarina Kruusval
Originally published in Sweden by Rabén & Sjögren under the title *Gubbar och galoscher!*
Library of Congress catalog card number: 00-135406
Printed in Denmark
First American edition, 2001
ISBN 91-29-65348-7

Lena Arro • Catarina Kruusval

BY GEEZERS AND GALOSHES!

R&S
BOOKS

Stockholm New York London Adelaide Toronto

One day the mail boat arrived, as usual, at the dock below the house where the old Granstrom brothers lived. This time, though, Mailman Johnny was not alone in the boat. He had a little boy with him.

"Who is that?" old man Granstrom asked.

"I don't know, but he is supposed to get off here," said Mailman Johnny.

Then he lifted the boy onto the dock.
  "Smelts and sardines!" old man
Granstrom exclaimed in surprise. "What
kind of sprat are you?"

"Read the note!" Mailman Johnny called out. Then he took off.
  Old man Granstrom walked around the boy. He noticed a
slip of paper pinned to the back of the boy's sweater. He leaned
forward and read:

DEAR OLD FOLKS:
THIS IS BUBBLE, YOUR GRANDNEPHEW. PLEASE LOOK
AFTER HIM FOR A WEEK WHILE WE ARE IN KARESUANDO.
LOVE, COUSIN VIOLA

At that moment, old man Granstrom's brother, Herring August, came down from the house. He, too, read the note.

"So you are Bubble," he said. "Welcome! Come along, I'll make you some pancakes."

Herring August and Bubble went up to the house.

Old man Granstrom just stood there, trying to think of ways to keep little boys amused. For a whole week!

He needn't have worried. When Bubble had finished his pancakes, he opened his bag and took out a large box.

"You can help me with this," Bubble said. "If you're careful."

The old men looked at the box. There was a picture of a sailing ship on the lid.

"It's a ship model kit," Herring August said, sounding interested. "We should be able to do this, considering how much time we have spent sailing the seas."

Bubble opened the box and emptied everything out on the table. There must have been close to a million pieces.

"SCUPPERS AND SCUTTLEBUTTS!" old man Granstrom groaned. "I've never seen a ship like this before."

"Here are the sails," Bubble said, unfolding some tiny white handkerchiefs.

"You are supposed to fit all the parts together," Herring August explained. "Part A goes together with part B, and part B with part C."

Old man Granstrom was rummaging among the pieces.

"All I can find is something that looks like a boom with a 'Y' on it."

"It's probably the yardarm," said Herring August. "I've found the mainmast."

The old men forgot everything except the ship model. Bubble went to bed at eight, but they didn't notice.

At midnight, they were finally finished.
They were very proud. The model looked
just like the picture.

At the bottom of the box, Herring August found a
little piece of paper.

"It says: FOR FULL SIZE, PLEASE PLACE MODEL
IN WATER. What does that mean?"

"I don't know," said old man Granstrom, yawning.
"It's time to turn in. Good night."

Herring August took the model down to the shore
and put it in the water, wedged between some rocks.
Then he also went to bed.

In the morning, the old men and Bubble had breakfast. As they were clearing the table, old man Granstrom happened to look out the window.

"BY GULLIVER'S GALOSHES!" he called out. "There is a sailing ship down by the dock!"

They hurried out to take a closer look at the ship.

"Whose could it be?" old man Granstrom wondered.

"I think it's the model," said Herring August. "It did say 'full size.'"

"Oh, goody!" said Bubble. "Can we be pirates?"

"It would be nice to go to sea again . . ." said Herring August. "Just for a little while."

Old man Granstrom cleared his throat and coughed a few times. "Well, why not?" he finally said.

"I'll be the captain, because it's my ship," Bubble said. "And you'll be the ship's cook." He pointed to old man Granstrom. "And Herring August can be up on the mast, keeping a lookout."

"I can't cook!" said old man Granstrom.

"Heights make me dizzy," said Herring August.

"I'm the captain, so I make the decisions," said Bubble.

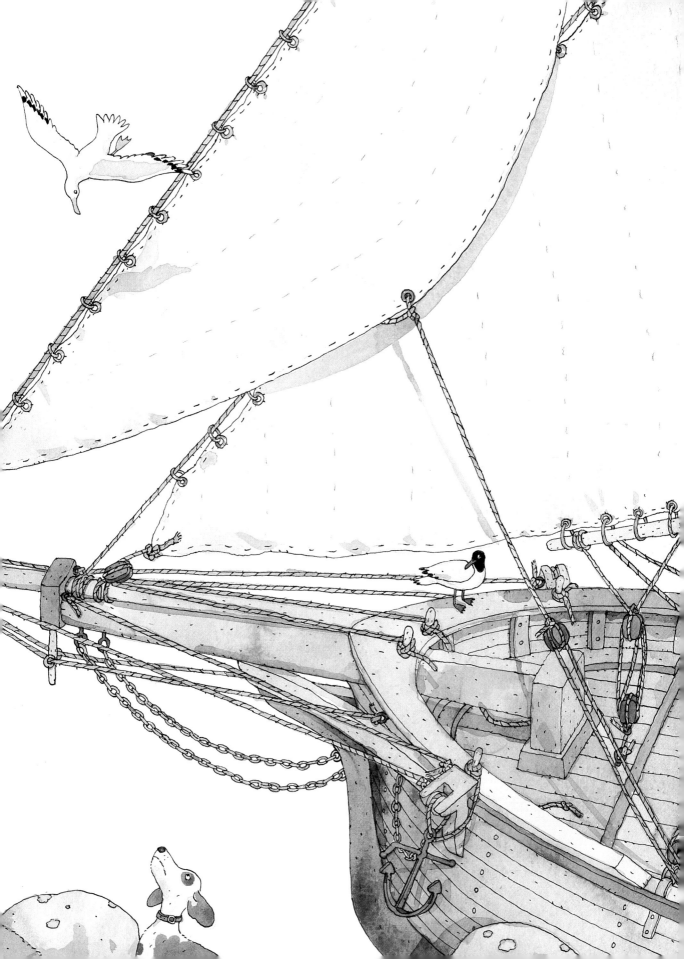

Bubble went out into the kitchen and got all the cans,
boxes of oatmeal, and bologna he could find. Then they
put the food in the wheelbarrow and loaded it on board.
"Anchors aweigh!" Bubble cried. "We're off!"

The first day, Herring August was up on the mast, hanging on for
dear life, feeling dizzy. Bubble was at the wheel, and old man
Granstrom tried to cook. From time to time, they could hear his
loud grumbling voice whenever something broke or burned.
"YOU RUBBERY RATTLESNAKE! I would turn you into hash
if only I knew *how*!" he shouted to the bologna, for example. And
when an egg slipped out of his hand and broke, he bellowed,
"YOU GLUTINOUS GLOWWORM!" and made the walls shake.

For dinner, they had burned potatoes with burned bologna, and eggs, burned on both sides.

Herring August was allowed to come down to eat, and he was happy about that.

When old man Granstrom had finished scraping all the black from his slice of bologna, he said, "The most terrible threats of the seven seas are nothing compared with frizzled bologna. This means mutiny!"

"What is mutiny?" Bubble asked.

"It's when you lock the captain in his cabin so you can do what you want!"

"You can't, because there's no key," Bubble said. "So there!"

In the evening, Bubble steered the ship into a cove between some high rocks.

"I want dessert," he said. "Herring August can make a raid onshore and bring back the booty."

Herring August took the dinghy and rowed ashore. Luckily, he found an ice-cream stand. He bought some ice cream and rowed back.

"Are you sure that this is really booty?" Bubble asked.

"In a way," Herring August answered.

The next day, they headed straight out to sea.

"I want to see the real ocean!" Bubble said. "With sharks and sea monsters and dangerous currents."

After they had been sailing for a long, long time, Bubble decided that now they were in the Pacific Ocean. Old man Granstrom pointed out a shark and something that was probably a sea monster.

Herring August was up on the mast, sunbathing. He was hardly dizzy at all and he was very happy not to be cooking.

"Look ahead!" he suddenly shouted. "Ship ahoy!"

Two women were waving at them from a small motorboat.

"Go ahead, board them and steal their treasure," Bubble said to old man Granstrom.

"Are you sure it's all right to do that?" asked old man Granstrom.

Bubble thought about it. "Maybe I had better do it myself. After all, I'm the captain – maybe I look more dangerous?"

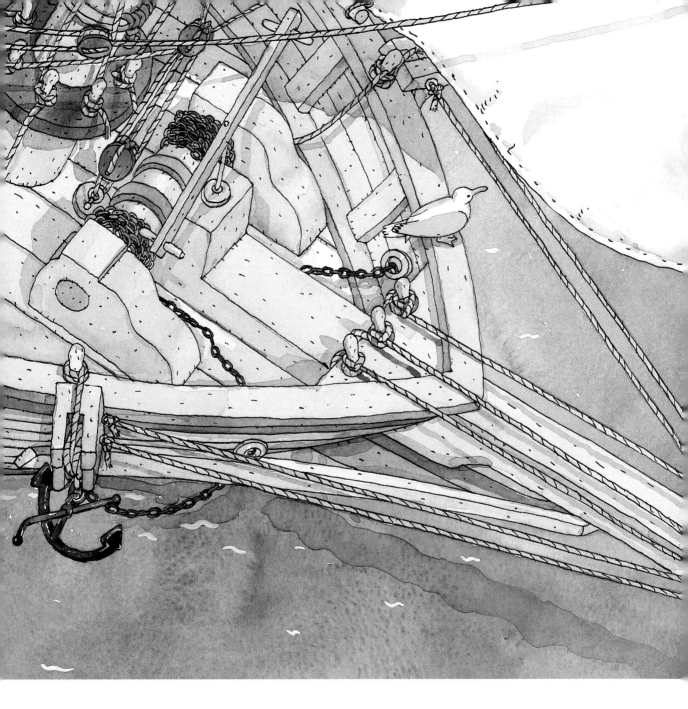

He climbed down the rope ladder to the motorboat. The women
did not seem particularly frightened. After a long while, Bubble
returned with a chocolate bar and a red pencil with an eraser.
   "They didn't have very much treasure," he said.
   The women waved goodbye as they sailed away.

Old man Granstrom got to be a pretty good cook.

He hardly ever burned anything, and he stopped making all that noise.

But they soon ran out of potatoes and bologna, so they had oatmeal soup and hard-boiled eggs, or hot oatmeal with white beans, or beans with egg soup.

Finally, there was nothing but oatmeal left. Then Bubble decided it was time to go home.

While Bubble steered the ship across the Indian Ocean, Herring August took a nap up on the mast. Old man Granstrom made dessert from what was left of the oatmeal. They finished it as they rounded the Cape of Good Hope.

When they were almost home, Bubble said, "Now we have sailed around the world."

"That's right," said old man Granstrom. "It was good to smell the sea air again. And you were really good at steering!"

"I have never served as a lookout for a better captain," said Herring August.

They tied up at the dock that belonged to the old
men and went ashore. Bubble gave a big yawn.
"I want to go to bed. You will have to dry the
ship off so that it shrinks enough to fit in the box
again."

"By all seafaring sea urchins!" old man Granstrom
exclaimed. "How do we do that?"

"How about bath towels?" Herring August
suggested.

"By geezers and galoshes! It's worth a try!" said old man
Granstrom.